The Museum Mice of Herne Bay

Summer Stories

By Mrs Mandy Mouse

Illustrations by Angela Kennedy

Editor-in-Chief Dianne Long

Published in association with the Seaside Museum, Herne Bay, 12 William Street, Herne Bay, Kent

@seasidemuseum   www.theseasidemuseum.org

Table of Contents

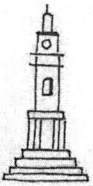

The Museum Mice Arrive

Once upon a time, Mrs Mouse was scampering across a field when she saw a poster in a hedge. It said Come To Sunny Herne Bay.

Mrs Mouse went home. She said

to Mr Mouse, 'I would like a holiday. I would like to go to Herne Bay.'

Her three children heard her.

Monty Mouse said, 'I would like a holiday. I would like to go to Herne Bay.'

Maisie Mouse said, 'I would like a holiday. I would like to go to Herne Bay.'

Max Mouse said, 'I would like a holiday. I would like to go to Herne

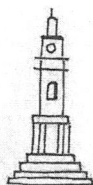

Bay.'

Mr Mouse said, 'What a good idea. We will all go to Herne Bay. Now, children, go and pack.'

So Monty Mouse packed his bucket and spade.

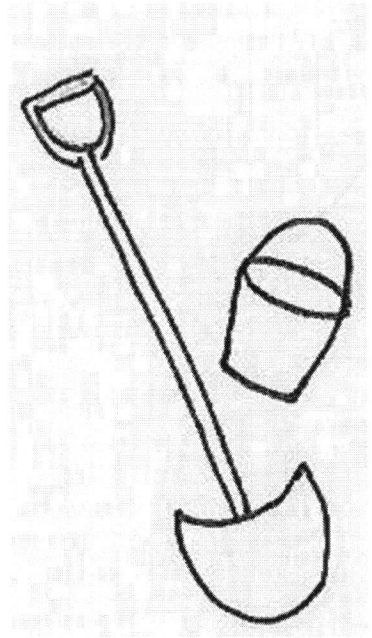

Maisie Mouse packed her bucket and spade.

Max Mouse packed his bucket

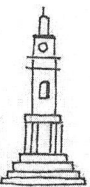

and spade.

'Don't forget your swimming costumes,' said Mrs Mouse.

So Monty Mouse packed his swimming costume.

Maisie Mouse packed her swimming costume.

Max Mouse packed his swimming costume.

At last they were ready.

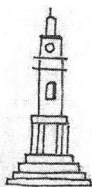

They all set off for Herne Bay.

When they had gone a little way, Monty Mouse said, 'Are we there yet?'

'Not yet,' said Mrs Mouse.

When they had gone a bit further, Maisie Mouse said, 'Are we there yet?'

'Not yet,' said Mrs Mouse.

When they had gone a bit further, Max Mouse said, 'Are we there yet?'

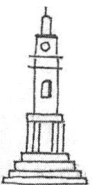

'Not yet,' said Mrs Mouse.

She turned to Mr Mouse.

'The children are getting tired,' she said. 'Let us stop for our picnic.'

They sat down in a field and Mr Mouse opened the picnic basket.

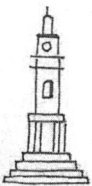

'What sort of sandwiches would you like, Monty?' asked Mrs Mouse. 'There are jam sandwiches and ham sandwiches and cheese sandwiches . . .'

'Cheese, please,' said Monty.

'What sort of sandwiches would you like, Maisie?' asked Mrs Mouse. 'There are jam sandwiches and ham sandwiches and cheese sandwiches . . .'

'Cheese, please,' said Maisie.

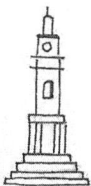

'What sort of sandwiches would you like, Max? There are jam sandwiches and ham sandwiches and cheese sandwiches . . '

'Cheese, please,' said Max.

Mrs Mouse gave them their sandwiches. Then she said to Mr Mouse, 'What sort of sandwiches would you like. There are jam

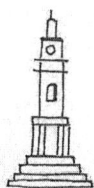

sandwiches and ham sandwiches.'

'I will have the jam sandwiches,' said Mr Mouse.

'Then I will have the ham sandwiches,' said Mrs Mouse.

They had just finished their picnic when a car stopped in the lane nearby.

A family of Big People got out.

There were two grown up Big People with a little boy and a little girl.

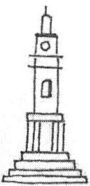

'Anna, Tom, you must help us
to set out the picnic,' said the grown
ups to the children.

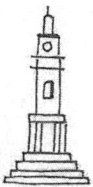

'I will set out the food,' said
Anna.

'I will set out the drinks,' said
Tom.

They opened their picnic
hamper and set out the food and
drink.

'I am glad we are going to
Herne Bay for our holiday,' said the
little girl.

'So am I,' said the little boy.

Mr and Mrs Mouse looked at

each other. Then they looked at their tired little mice. Then they looked at the car.

The back door was open.

'Come on, this car will take us all the way to Herne Bay. But you must be very quiet,' said Mr Mouse.

'As quiet as mice!' said Mrs Mouse.

Mr and Mrs Mouse packed away their picnic. Monty, Maisie and Max helped.

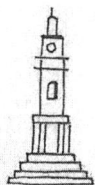

Then they all scurried towards the car and jumped inside. All except Max, who could not jump high enough.

He gave a squeal as he fell down.

Anna and Tom heard him.

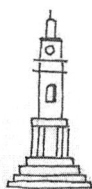

'Look! There are some mice climbing into the car,' said Anna.

'We are going on holiday, but our legs are tired,' said Max. 'We would like to go in your car. We are going to Herne Bay.'

Anna laughed. She lifted Max up and put him in the car.

Max thanked her.

When the Big People had eaten their picnic they returned to the car. Then they all set off for Herne Bay.

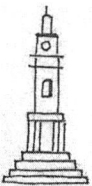

To Herne Bay

It was a long journey. The mice were tired when they got there.

The car stopped in a road outside a blue building. The building had a low window with lots of interesting things to look at.

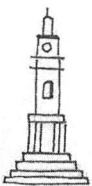

'We need somewhere to stay,' said Mr Mouse.

'This place looks nice,' said Mrs Mouse. 'We could stay here.'

Monty Mouse was learning to read. He looked at the writing on the front of the building then he read it aloud.

'The Seaside Museum,' he said.

Maisie read the next part of the writing. 'Herne Bay.'

Mrs Mouse beamed with pride.

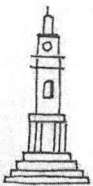

She liked having clever children
who could read and write.

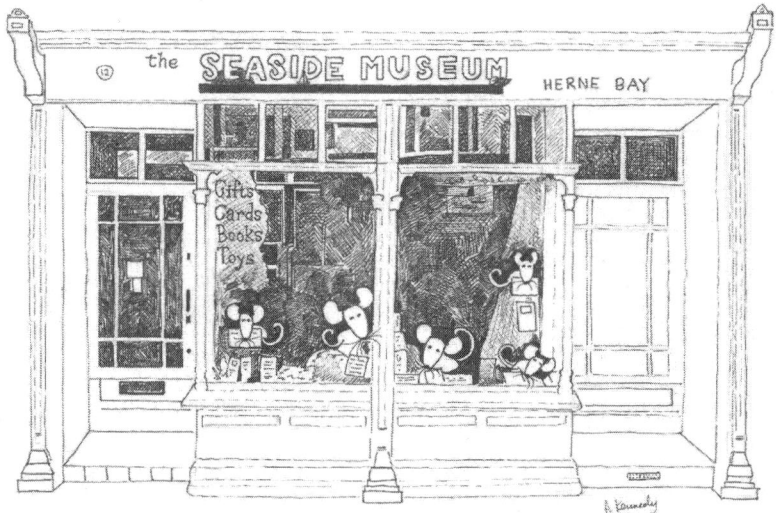

Max was too little to be able to
read and write just yet, so he
squeaked instead.

Mrs Mouse jumped up onto the

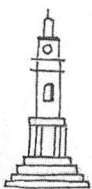

window ledge and looked at all the lovely things on display.

'Those shells look like little beds. They are just the right size for us,' she said.

Mr Mouse led the way inside.

There were two Big People at the counter and three more Big People looking round the museum.

'We are closing now,' said one of the Big People at the counter.

Monty Mouse turned to go.

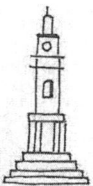

'Only Big People have to leave,' said Mrs Mouse. 'Be quiet now, children. Quiet as mice.'

The Big People started to leave the museum. At last they had all gone. All except one of the ladies at the counter who was making it all tidy. Then she went too. She locked the door behind her.

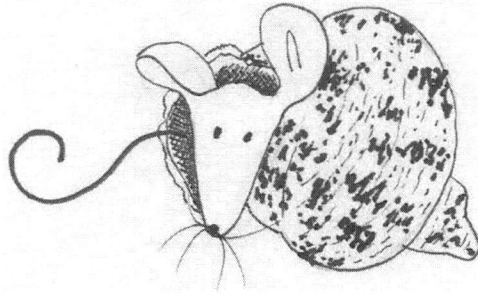

Mrs Mouse chose the nicest

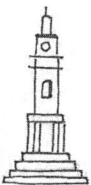

shells. She turned them into little
mice beds with little blankets and
little pillows.

Monty Mouse yawned. Maisie
Mouse yawned. Max Mouse
yawned. It had been a tiring day.

Mrs Mouse said to her children,
'Time for bed.'

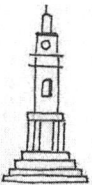

'When can we go swimming?' asked Monty.

'Tomorrow,' said Mrs Mouse.

'When can we play with our buckets and spades?' asked Maisie.

'Tomorrow,' said Mrs Mouse.

'When can we . . .'

But Max never finished his sentence, because he fell asleep!

'I think we are going to like it here,' said Mrs Mouse.

'So do I,' said Mr Mouse. 'This

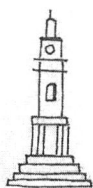

will be our new home. We are not field mice any longer. We are town mice.'

Mrs Mouse said, 'We are museum mice! The museum mice of Herne Bay.'

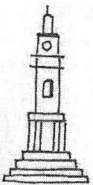

The Museum Mice in Summer

Once upon a time, Mr Mouse looked out of the museum window and saw the sun was shining.

'Do you remember why we came to Herne Bay?' he asked.

'We came for a holiday,' said Mrs Mouse. 'But then we liked it so much we stayed.'

'I think we should treat today as

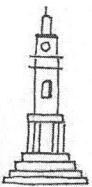

a holiday,' said Mr Mouse. 'The sun is shining. I think we will go to the beach.'

'Hooray,' said Monty.

'Hooray,' said Maisie.

'Hooray,' said Max.

'What a good idea,' said Mrs Mouse. 'I would like to go to the beach. I have not been to the beach in a long time.'

'Don't forget your fishing nets,' said Mr Mouse.

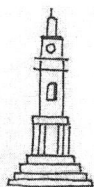

'We won't,' said the little mice.

'Now, children, go and pack,' said Mrs Mouse.

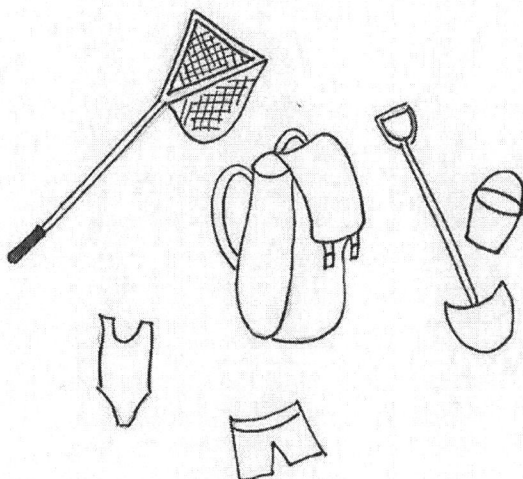

Monty fetched his rucksack.

Maisie fetched her rucksack.

Max fetched his rucksack.

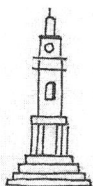

'Don't forget your swimming costumes,' said Mrs Mouse.

Monty packed his swimming costume. Maisie packed her swimming costume. Max packed his swimming costume.

At last they had packed everything. They were ready. They all set off for the beach.

It seemed a very long way to the little mice.

They soon came to the road.

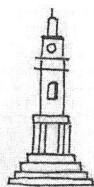

'Stay close, children,' said Mr Mouse.

'We must use the zebra crossing,' said Mrs Mouse.

'Where is the zebra?' asked

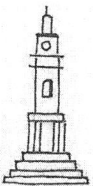

Monty.

'I can not see the zebra,' said Maisie Mouse.

'Nor can I,' said Max Mouse.

'It is not a real zebra,' said Mr Mouse. 'It is a place where we can cross the road in safety. It has black and white markings to help us find it.'

They found the zebra crossing. The little mice waited at the side of the road but the cars did not stop.

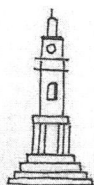

'They can not see us. We are too small,' said Mrs Mouse.

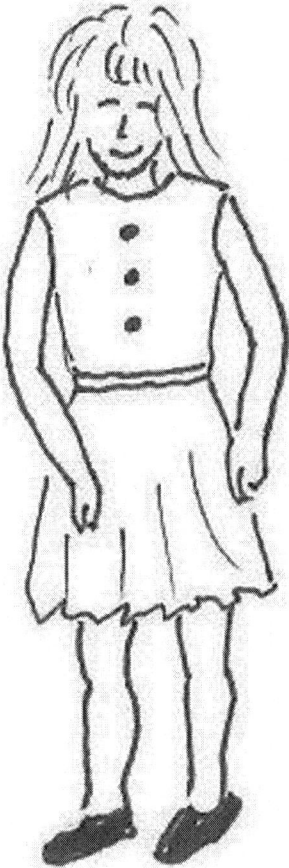

Just then a family of Big People came up. Max recognised them. They were the same Big People who had driven the car to Herne Bay.

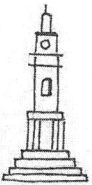

'Hold my hand, Anna,' said Anna's mummy to the little girl.

Anna held her mummy's hand.

Tom was there, too.

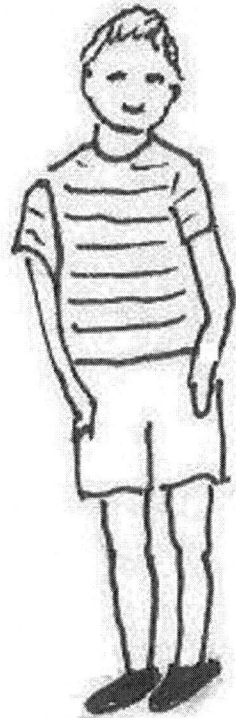

'Hold my hand, Tom,' said Tom's daddy to the little boy.

Tom held his daddy's hand.

'Hello Anna. Hello, Tom,'

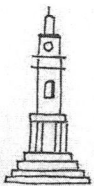

called Max.

The children looked down and saw him. They waved. The museum mice waved back.

Anna bent down. She said, 'Jump into my pocket and I will help you to cross the road.'

So the museum mice jumped into her pocket.

The cars stopped for the Big People. Anna and Tom crossed the road with their mummy and daddy.

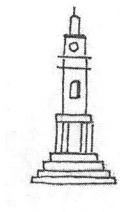

The museum mice crossed the road with them.

Anna bent down and the museum mice jumped out of her pocket.

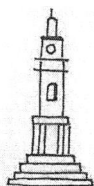

'Where are you going?' asked Anna.

'We are going to the beach,' said Max.

Tom said, 'We are going to look at the statue of Amy Johnson.'

The museum mice thanked them and waved goodbye. Then they scampered down to the beach.

There were lots of pebbles on the beach. They looked like enormous boulders to the mice.

Monty climbed on top of one of the pebbles.

'Look at me!' he said.

Maisie and Max laughed to see him.

'I will take a picture,' said Mrs

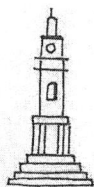

Mouse.

She had a tiny mouse camera on her tiny mouse phone.

'Look at me!' said Maisie, as she joined Monty.

'Look at – oops!' said Max.

He could not climb on to the pebble because he was too small.

Mr Mouse lifted him up.

Max stood on the pebble with Monty and Maisie.

Monty, Maisie and Max smiled

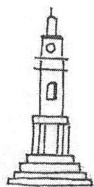

and waved. Mrs Mouse took a picture.

'Just one more,' said Mrs Mouse.

Monty stood on one leg to show off. He began to wobble.

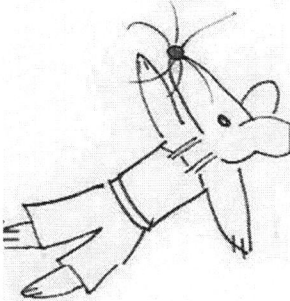

Monty clutched at Maisie, and Maisie began to wobble.

Maisie clutched at Max, and Max began to wobble.

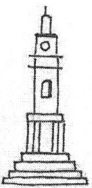

Mrs Mouse took the picture, just as the children fell off the pebble boulder.

Luckily, no one was hurt and they all laughed.

'We cannot swim here. This part of the sea is for jet skis,' said Mr Mouse. 'We must move further along.'

They scampered along the beach. When they reached a safe spot they found a tiny patch of sand.

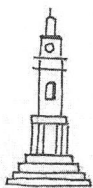

Monty, Maisie and Max began to build a sand castle. They all helped each other. The sand was damp. Just right for building with!

Soon it was very big, or at least it seemed big to the mice!

It had towers and a moat.

They ran to the sea and filled their buckets with water. Then they poured the water in the moat.

The moat was just the right size for a mouse swimming pool.

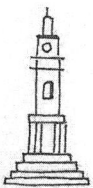

Monty jumped in and started to swim.

Maisie jumped in and started to swim.

Max jumped in and started to swim.

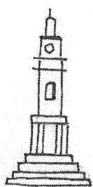

'Ah! This is the life,' said Mr Mouse as he lay on the beach, soaking up the sun.

Mrs Mouse was sunbathing too.

Monty, Maisie and Max were soon tired after their swimming. They climbed out of the moat and sat beside Mrs Mouse. They looked at the picnic hamper.

'I am hungry,' said Monty.

'I am hungry,' said Maisie.

'I am hungry,' said Max.

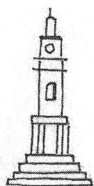

Mrs Mouse opened the picnic hamper.

'What sort of sandwiches would you like, Monty?' asked Mrs Mouse. 'There are jam sandwiches and ham sandwiches and cheese sandwiches . . .'

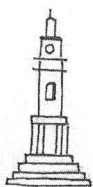

'Cheese, please,' said Monty.

'What sort of sandwiches would you like, Maisie?' asked Mrs Mouse. 'There are jam sandwiches and ham sandwiches and cheese sandwiches . . .'

'Cheese, please,' said Maisie.

'What sort of sandwiches would you like, Max? There are jam sandwiches and ham sandwiches and cheese sandwiches . . .'

'Cheese, please,' said Max.

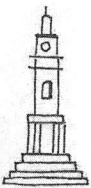

Mrs Mouse gave them their sandwiches.

Then she said to Mr Mouse, 'What sort of sandwiches would you like. There are jam sandwiches and ham sandwiches.'

'I will have the jam sandwiches,' said Mr Mouse.

'Then I will have the ham sandwiches,' said Mrs Mouse.

She gave everyone some lemonade to drink.

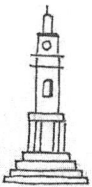

After their picnic, the mice took their fishing nets down to the sea. The tide was out and they paddled in the shallow water.

Monty put his fishing net in the water.

Maisie put her fishing net in the water.

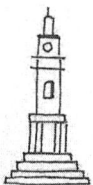

Max put his fishing net in the water.

But they did not catch anything!

At last it was time to go home.

The little mice gathered their belongings together. They went back to the zebra crossing. They had to wait a long time for the cars to stop. At last the road was clear and the museum mice scampered across.

'I had a good day today,' said Monty Mouse with a small yawn, as

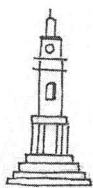

they went back to the museum.

'I had a good day today,' said Maisie Mouse with a big yawn, as they went inside.

But Max Mouse did not say anything. He was asleep!

'Time for bed, children,' said Mrs Mouse.

Monty and Maisie did not

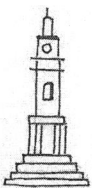

argue. They were tired after all their fresh air. They crept slowly up the stairs.

Mr Mouse picked Max up and carried him to bed.

They curled up in their little mouse beds. Then they said goodnight to each other.

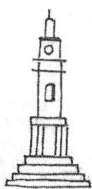

Very soon they were all fast asleep.

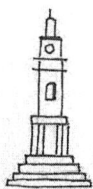

Amy Johnson's Statue

One day, Maisie Mouse found a poster in the museum. It had a picture of Amy Johnson on it. It said that Amy Johnson was a famous woman who had flown a lot of planes.

'There is a statue of Amy Johnson in Herne Bay. Can we go to see it?' asked Maisie.

Mr and Mrs Mouse said, 'Yes.'

'We will all go,' said Mr
Mouse.

They put on their coats and
went outside. They scampered over
to the zebra crossing. There were
lots of cars zooming down the road.

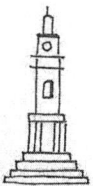

At last the cars stopped and they were able to cross.

They walked along the promenade towards the statue. As they did so, they passed the clock tower.

'What time is it?' asked Mr Mouse.

Monty could tell the time.

'It is ten o'clock,' he said.

'Good,' said Mr Mouse.

'Look,' said Maisie. 'There is

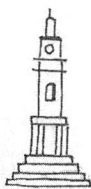

Tom.'

'And there is Anna,' said Max.

The little mice waved to Tom and Anna. Tom and Anna waved back.

Then the mice scampered along the promenade.

They passed the bandstand.

'I like the bandstand,' said Monty.

'So do I,' said Maisie.

'I like it, too,' said Max. 'One

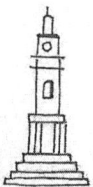

day we can come and listen to a
band.'

They scampered on until they
reached the statue of Amy Johnson.
They had to dodge a lot of Big
People on the way!

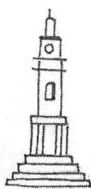

'I can see the statue,' called Monty.

'So can I,' said Maisie.

'Where is it?' asked Max.

He was so little he could not see it.

Mr Mouse lifted him up.

'Oh, now I can see it,' said Max. 'But I still can not see it very well.

Mr Mouse put Max on his shoulders.

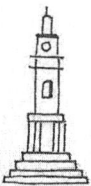

Max could see even better.

They soon reached the statue. It was made out of bronze and it was gleaming in the sunshine.

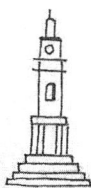

Max climbed down and ran around the statue. It was very interesting. Amy was smiling and looking out to sea.

'Amy Johnson is famous,' said Mrs Mouse. 'She flew all over the world. She even flew to Australia, and that is a very long way away.'

'I wish I could fly a plane,' said Max.

'It would have to be a very small plane,' said Monty.

'What has she got on her head?' asked Maisie.

'They are flying goggles,' said Mr Mouse. 'They help her to see when she is flying.'

'She looks very happy,' said Max.

'That is because she likes flying,' said Mrs Mouse.

Monty put his arms out and pretended to be a plane. He ran around Amy's feet, making a noise

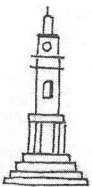

like a plane.

Maisie put her arms out and pretended to be a plane. She ran around Amy's feet, making a noise like a plane.

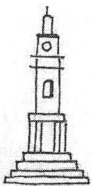

Max put his arms out and pretended to be a plane. He ran around Amy's feet, making a noise like a plane.

At last the little mice were tired. Monty fell down. Maisie fell down on top of him. Max fell down on top of them. They all laughed.

'Time to go home,' said Mr Mouse.

The little mice were tired as they walked back to the museum. Max was so tired, Mr Mouse had to carry him.

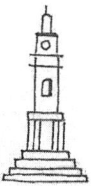

When they got back to the museum, there were lots of children there. The children liked to visit the museum because there were lots of interesting things to see and do.

The mice had to be very quiet as they scampered upstairs. Quiet as mice!

Then they went into their own little mouse hole. It looked very nice. Mrs Mouse had decorated it. Mr Mouse had made some furniture.

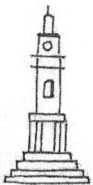

There was a spoon for Mr and Mrs Mouse to sleep in.

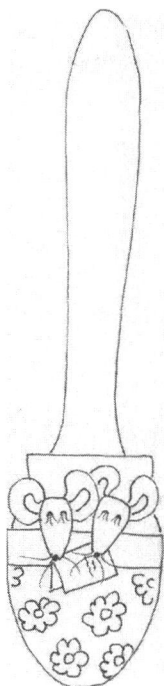

There were walnut shells and oyster shells for the children to sleep in.

There was a cupboard for the buckets and spades. There was a table and some chairs.

They all sat down and had some cheese to eat. They had some milk to drink.

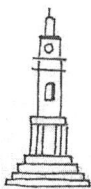

The little mice had a rest. Then, when they were not tired any longer, they went downstairs to see what the children were doing.

The children were talking about Amy Johnson and they were making paper planes.

Soon it was time for the children to go home. They tidied their tables and went over to the door.

'Look! I can see Tom and

Anna!' said Max.

He waved to them. Anna did not see him. She was saying goodbye to Mrs Long. But Tom saw him and Tom waved back.

Max scampered across the floor.

'No, Max! Come back!' called Monty. 'Mrs Long will see you!'

But it was too late. Tom was lifting Max up and putting him into one of the paper aeroplanes.

'Look at me!' Max squeaked. 'I am just like Amy Johnson. I can fly!'

Tom picked up the paper aeroplane and waved it around his head. Max was sitting inside it. He made an engine noise and pretended to fly the plane.

Just then, Mrs Long turned

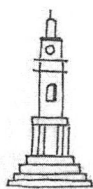

2

65

towards Tom.

Tom dropped the aeroplane.

Max Mouse scampered out.

Tom picked up the aeroplane
and put it in his bag.

Mrs Long looked puzzled. She

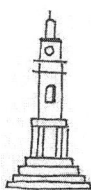

scratched her head.

'That is funny,' she said. 'I thought I saw a mouse, scampering out of the plane.'

'I think you must have imagined it,' said Tom. 'Mice can not fly planes.'

'Perhaps you are right,' said Mrs Long.

She said goodbye to the children.

Monty, Maisie and Max

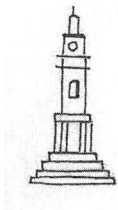

scampered upstairs. They were careful so that Mrs Long did not see them.

'Let us all make paper planes,' said Maisie.

'That is a good idea,' said Mr and Mrs Mouse.

The little mice made their own paper planes.

Maisie pretended to fly to Australia.

Monty pretended to fly to

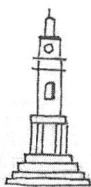

America.

But Max did not pretend to fly anywhere. He was fast asleep!

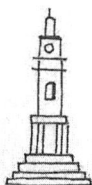

42551422R00043

Printed in Poland
by Amazon Fulfillment
Poland Sp. z o.o., Wrocław